GW01219536

Copyright © 2024 Authors as listed
All rights reserved. This book or any portion thereof may not be reproduced or used in any manner whatsoever without the express written permission of the publisher except for the use of brief quotations in a book review.

Printed in Spain by Club Hemingway VLC
First Printing, July 2024
ISBN 9798329432404

@clubhemingwayvlc

CLUB HEMINGWAY VLC

ANTHOLOGY I

HEMINGWAY HAIKU

more than just a club
it's a community of
expats and poets

- ***Richard Wallen***

CONTENTS

An Introduction from
CLUB HEMINGWAY VLC FOUNDER

Cate Baum

There is something about the written word that comes alive when it is spoken. Human beings have an innate love of listening to stories; first they listened round fires in the night, and now, in the form of audiobooks, podcasts, and of course, the ever-popular literary open mic events.

Club Hemingway was an idea I had for foreigners from all around the world now living in Valencia to come together with the common interest of telling stories in a common tongue: English. It's lonely to be living in another country, not always by choice, in a broken, warring world, and it's important to have ways of seeking out like-minded people, because it's hard to make connections in life at the best of times, and let's face it, writers, a lone wolf breed by nature, need extra help when it comes to talking to other humans.

Ernest Hemingway, the American writer and our namesake, came to Spain from the US in the 1920s to discover the country's obsession with bullfighting and boats, but the place he loved was Valencia. From La Pepica beach restaurant where he stayed in Malvarrosa, to the Hotel Inglés in the Ciutat Vella, to the Palacio Del Marqués de Dos Aguas where he took his wife Hadley in 1925, Hemingway was very fond of this city. He attended boozy gatherings just like our humble club at Radio City, (known in Castellano as *tertulias)*, was photographed by my friend Paco Cano (the legendary Valencian photographer who lived to be 102 years old, most famous for his coverage of the literal gory death of the bullfighter Manolete at Linares), and generally made a nuisance of himself about town.

Hemingway is often regarded as a 'terrible' person with disturbing behaviour not only in life, but also in his work: bullfighting folk spit that he made up words for *tauromaquía* while claiming to be an expert, and his cruelty to both animals and women is well-documented. But his nickname, the *guiri loco* *(*the crazy foreigner), strikes a chord for me. In the ever-present shadow of Franco's dictatorship, the 'different' people: the creatives, non-white, LGBTIA+, and disabled are still pushed out in certain corners of this country (although this is certainly changing).

As immigrants of all situations, ages and backgrounds, we relate to the feeling of being 'outside', even when we think we're 'in'. Maybe this is a common experience when living abroad, but I have felt it more acutely here in Valencia than anywhere else in Spain.

I paraphrase, but there is a Spanish saying about Valencians, that although they will open their arms to you, they will never close them around you. Unfortunately, many of us find ourselves on this edge, even after decades of attempting to fit in with groups of Valencians that have known each other all their lives. We never quite make the grade: we don't speak Valenciano, we don't know all the tiny, exacting customs of Fallas or paella. We didn't go to school together.

And so, passing the 'guiris go home' graffiti on the street walls, we nervously attend the sweaty bars of Ruzafa and Carmen for 'expat' meetups (ugh I hate that word 'expat'), those *intercambios* meant for learning Castellano to a decent level (ugh, I hate intercambios), and then we attempt to speak it only to be met with the judgement that we don't speak any Spanish at all! Or worse, we get asked why we don't speak Valenciano. Well, we might speak three or more languages already, *xe*! Give us a chance!

In Valencia, speaking English (a much simpler play) well enough to find a small hub of friends from wherever else becomes the only way of finding happiness.

And yes, we could flee for the Southern wilds: the rougher, passionate life of Andalusia with its majestic mountains, dull ports and dusty golf courses. We could brave the rain and political storms of the cruel Northern green, the deserts of Almeria, with its immigration issues and sea of plastic. The fierce life of the cities of Barcelona and Madrid most of us have already abandoned because we didn't like the pollution, pollen, or pickpockets. Haven't we guiris already ruined Benidorm?

We may never really feel at home in Spain, and it's hard to explain to Valencians why we can't go back to our own countries. Most of us will never return to where we were born. Some of us, like me, can't even really explain why.

And I do feel, reading over the pieces in this book, that most of us are feeling broken, or healing, or in flight; working through emotions in our writing that are incredibly important to understanding who we are, a way of letting it out to find an identity, a place in this world, whether it be through analysis of everyday events, or imagining situations or relationships, or recalling incidents and rolling them into autofiction.

Because stories are a survival mechanism. They are innate in us because they give us an opportunity to live other lives, to try dangerous or unknown situations on for size and see where they go. When we sat around fires back when we lived in caves and died in our twenties from toothache and childbirth and had to kill our own food with sticks, stories about others doing heroic and godly things proved that we survive when we share stories, because we get to find out, vicariously, what happens at the end.

Most of us have found something special here in Valencia, and lately at Hemingway, we've begun to attract Spanish members, maybe the more creative, 'different' people, who seamlessly fit into our scene, producing wonderful work in English. The laidback atmosphere in this city means creative life can flourish for us, if only we make the effort to share our ideas.

I hope that I have provided a campfire of sorts with Club Hemingway VLC, and in this book, our first anthology, we start with an apt poem about this feeling of trying to belong.

Welcome to the *guiri loco* world of Club Hemingway VLC!

THE LONELY EXPAT

Sandhya Devas

In an unknown land
Far away from home
Navigating an unknown tongue
A foreigner's tale of woe.

It's a crisp cold morning
The smell of coffee permeates the air
The church bells ring incessantly
With not a care.
Yet the morning symphony
Brings a sense of calm
A feeling I have not found elsewhere
A foreign city's charm!

Sipping on coffee
Sitting on cobble stoned streets
Watching the world go by
And nodding to random greets.

The quest is real
To find a connection
At craft workshops and coffee meets
Among the many I vibe
I still struggle to find my tribe.

Strangers have become friends
Good friends a few,
Some endure like kin
A few have faded away too.

There is yet a sense of joy
In living in this distant land
Of an adventure unseen
Exploring the art & architecture
It's culture and cuisine.

But this wanderlust mind
Of savouring different lands
Comes with a cost so dear
In this land I call home
I will always be a
Lonely expat, I fear!

IT'S COMING HOME

Brian Kelly

Look what's coming home.

It was always going to be problematic. Supporting England. Cheering for the young lions. First, there's the Irish thing. Six hundred years. The old enemy. *Tiocfaidh ár lá.* Then there's the yobs. It's coming home. Our home. Go home. Back where you came from etcetera. But, you know, the missus is plastic. London Irish. English. And my daughter, who pronounces her THs and corrects me when I mispronounce dis and dat, is English too.

So yeah, we go to my mate's BBQ. Big screen out the back. Beers on ice. Huddled under the gazebo when the rain comes down, but happy to be together. Getting drunk in flesh rather than on Zoom. It starts with the anthems. The Italian number full of... well, Italian-ness. Then "God Save the Queen". The lions arm in arm. Proclaiming their loyalty to the matriarch. A woman whose bloodline runs through all the old aristocratic families of Europe.

The ref does the toss. England to kick off, but before they do: the knee. At the BBQ nobody says anything. Maybe ITV is editing the sound. Maybe there aren't any boos this time. I'd read an article a few weeks ago criticising the gesture. This is not America. What does taking the knee mean in a British context? Subverting knighthood? Half of them already have MBEs for doing very little indeed. It was all very clever. The kind of intellectual smokescreen that pretends not to understand the moral impetus behind an action of solidarity. If the lads on the terrace, coked up to their tits, were booing for reasons related to semiotic fidelity, you'd have to call that rapid intellectual progress. The players stand up and the game begins.

Six minutes later, a roar ripples across London. Different internet speeds. The fibre crowd, fifty quid a month, throw their champagne skywards. Then your standard broadband gang are in on the action, craft beer flying this way and that. Sitting in the rain at the back of a Barnet semi-d,we get to see Shawdo his thing about thirty seconds later.

It's coming home. The spirit of '66. The cliches are coming thick and fast. Come on England.

At half-time, Dave shows me some videos of Trafalgar Square. Lads snorting gear on camera. Bucket hat doing little to obscure his face from coming joblessness.Oh shit. Rob's got a video to show too. A bunch of hooligans rushing the gates at Wembley. Middle-aged men with expensive beer bellies and cheap tattoos kicking each other on the ground. On the telly, Gary Lineker is excited. Gary Neville believes. Roy Keane...well, he does his Roy Keane thing. The second half starts and Italy are on top.

You can see what's happening from here. The wingbacks are being pinned and the back three is becoming a five. But Southgate, the old defender, the man who missed that peno in '96, he's reluctant to make a change. He's conservative until they inevitably concede and only then rings the changes. Four at the back. Henderson on. Then at the end of extra time, with penalties on their way: Henderson back off again.

On come Rashford, Sancho and Saxa. They barely kicked a ball all tournament and he brings them on now? Is this Southgate saving his defensive players from the penalty miss that haunts him at night? Everyone at the BBQ groans.

But at first, it goes well. Up comes Harry. Bang! Back of the net! Then Italy miss. The greasy fucking gangster puts it straight into Pickford's paws. Maguire comes up next. And you're looking at the big concrete head on him and you think this is going high and wide, but no, like a rocket, straight into the top corner. Two-nil up. It's coming home. Italy score their next and then you realise what Southgate's done. He's left the three young black kids for the end. He wants England's victory to be a victory over racism. And you watch Rashford come up to the spot. And you can almost hear the racists stretching their Twitter fingers. The feeder of children. A future Knight of the Realm.

But deep down in their Imperialist souls they still want him to miss. And you think to yourself, What has Southgate done? Why put these young men under this ridiculous pressure?

As Marcus begins his run up, you just know he can feel the fuckers pissing on Nelson's Column and racking up lines on the fourth plinth, the one they kept for the Queen for when she died, the matriarch whose bloodlines remained as white as their cocaine, now they've run that little princess of Woke back to the colonies.

Rashford misses. Of course he does. Who can strike a ball true with all that stinking history hung around your neck? And now you wish someone from The Guardian would intervene. Get Kay Tempest to rewrite the script. Get Steve McQueen to do the shoot. But it doesn't happen that way and Sancho and Saxa miss too.

Everyone at the BBQ groans. Tears on the TV screen. Gareth's responsibility. Solidarity with the young lions. Only one year till the World Cup.

In twelve little months, God knows what'll come home.

I DID MY HAPPY DANCE WHEN I PUT ON WEIGHT

Marla Stein

I love bread!

While I'm an equal opportunity fan of these carbs, some of my favorites are focaccia, Italian, and New York everything bagels. Who am I kidding? I'll pretty much eat any bread fresh out of the oven.

Along with savoring the delicious smell, there's nothing like tearing into a warm loaf. While I enjoy eating bread plain, I also love dipping it in oil, pesto, or even hummus. It doesn't matter as it always tastes amazing. And, thanks to its soft texture, each bite always feels like a warm hug that, (if only for a few moments), makes everything seem better.

Bread is instant gratification and I'm not ashamed to admit that it's been my companion more times than I care to count. It's even helped pick up my spirits when I've been in a funk, lonely, stressed, and bored.

Yes, I know my love of bread makes me an emotional eater. I'm also aware that thanks to my obsession with these carbs, I've put on more than my share of unwanted weight over the years.

Bread Has Been a Source of Comfort During Tough Times

While I'm grateful to have friends and family I can rely on when the going gets rough, bread too has been a default that has helped me through difficult situations.

Let me explain…

I was diagnosed with breast cancer over 20 years ago. Along with processing this life-shattering news when I was 32, I needed a lot of help navigating the journey I was forced to go on. While my inner circle checked in regularly and attended doctor appointments with me, I also craved foods that I was able to tolerate and brought me comfort.

If you've ever experienced chemotherapy, I'm sure you're aware that the chemicals pumped into you can take a massive toll on your body. These drugs can do a number on your tastebuds as well.

As part of my breast cancer treatment, I went through chemotherapy and surgery for a bilateral mastectomy. In addition to going through four rounds of Adriamycin and Cytoxan (AC) – the kind of chemo that makes your hair fall out – I struggled to find foods that didn't taste like metal. So, I turned to chocolate, pasta, and bread. Yes, while indulging in a carb overload wasn't the healthiest choice, I didn't care. I was just happy that it was easy to digest and tasted good!

I gained 18 pounds when I went through treatment. But, thanks to the comfort of bread and other carb-based foods, I got through one of the most difficult times in my life.

###

In January 2020, I left the States for an epic adventure to Spain, Italy, Morocco, and Portugal. Like everyone else, my plans were derailed when the pandemic hit in March. So, instead of gallivanting overseas, I ended up spending three months living in Lisbon during lockdown.

My time in Portugal was an unexpected and isolating experience. Since I'm pretty good at adapting, I quickly learned to cope with the COVID crisis by joining online communities, working on creative projects, and spending plenty of time trying different types of Portuguese food.

I was thrilled to discover that locals love toast sandwiches. Avocado, eggs, hummus, meat — you name it, it goes on toast.

Once I tried the bread used to make this common Portuguese meal, I was hooked. So, it's no surprise that I eventually had a hard time buttoning my jeans.

On the days it rained during the lockdown in Lisbon, I would grab a piece of bread with hummus, lightly toast it, and then quickly devour it. When it was sunny and safe to go outdoors, I'd start my day dipping bread into something yummy, put on a mask, and then venture outside for the short period we were allowed to be on the street. Understandably, food had become my companion and source of comfort during this unprecedented time.

While in Portugal, I did my best to adjust. However, processing a global health crisis in an unfamiliar environment was a bit daunting at times. Thanks to my love of carbs and adventurous pallet, it became a little easier. And so, when I got back to the States and jumped on the scale, I wasn't completely devastated to see I was nine pounds heavier than before the pandemic. Instead, I celebrated getting through a difficult time by doing my happy dance.

###

A few months after making a long-awaited move abroad, I was diagnosed with a rare form of cancer called Neuroendocrine

Tumors (NETS) in my lungs. Unsurprisingly, this earth-shattering news rattled me to the core. In addition to having to navigate a healthcare system in a foreign country, I've been forced to mourn the life I envisioned. Rather than dream about traveling and making tons of social plans, I've had to work on accepting that there's currently no cure for my chronic disease. And once again, I've had to revisit my relationship with food and the number on the scale.

When I received my second cancer diagnosis, my obsession with bread was under control. In times of crisis, I quickly realized that sometimes you have to go against the grain (pun intended) and do things that work for you; regardless if it means putting more curves on your body.

One of the worst things to tell a cancer patient is that they look like they've lost weight – particularly if it comes across as a compliment. Trust me, a sick person doesn't need to be reminded that they are ill – especially if it's from someone who knows their situation.

While I eat what I can, when I can, it's a challenge. Every day, I'm forced to make appealing food choices that have the most nutritional benefits and won't upset my system. Finding foods that are high in protein, low in sugar, and with the right type of fiber is exhausting and frustrating. Figuring out what I can put in my body has also led to unintentional weight loss.

Although my current situation has rattled me to the core, it's forced me to be both proactive and gentle with myself. Now, I'm slowly discovering what works so I'm able to maintain a healthy weight.

###

Living through a pandemic, surviving breast cancer, and dealing with stage four cancer are all reminders that tomorrow isn't promised. So, while I've gained and struggled with extra pounds during times of crisis – it's all good.

It's more important that I get to do my happy dance, regardless of the number on the scale.

IT ALL COMES ROUND AGAIN

Dominique Downs

TRIBALISM
MATRIARCHY
PATRIARCHY
THEOCRACY
AUTOCRACY
MONARCHY
ARISTOCRACY
OLIGARCHY
PLUTOCRACY
DICTATORSHIP
MILITARISM
CAPITALISM
SOCIALISM
COMMUNISM
FASCISM
ANARCHY
DEMOCRACY
MERITOCRACY
CONSUMERISM
TECHNOCRACY
CORPORATOCRACY
CRONYISM
PATHOCRACY
KAKISTOCRACY
IDIOCRACY
TRIBALISM

CAMERA SHY

Henry Baum

"I'm so glad I met you,"

She looked beautiful. She looked like a princess, in a white low-cut gown, but not too low cut, and her hair up, a couple strands falling on the shoulders. She was accepting an award. She had won best actress. She was saying, "I love you," to her new husband.

I went to high school with her. We were Chemistry lab partners. She was beautiful then, always a princess. Diplomatic too. Popular but nice to me. Sort of condescending, but in a way that I was grateful for it. We were sort of friends, at least in chemistry class. We did a report together. I don't remember what it was about. We had to get in front of class. Halfway through, my hands were shaking so much I couldn't hold the index cards with my notes. People in class were mimicking my shaking hands. I looked over at Robin who gave me a pitying look, a warm, motherly kind of look.

"Well," she said. And then she gave the entire report herself. She was confident even then. We were given a C because of me. It was one of the worst moments in high school and the one that's stuck with me the most. Those kids mocking my shaking hands.

"I'm so glad I met you."

She was talking about her husband, Tim Griffith. They didn't show him but everyone knew who she was talking about.

She looked like the most happy a person could be. I've seen all her movies.

Two years later I ran into her. At the supermarket where I work. I'm a manager but it's still only a supermarket so I was a little embarrassed to see her.

Sandra came up to me. I was in my office tucked back from the market. It still smelled like a refrigerator. Same lighting as the market. Bright so you could see the products.

Sandra came in filling up the doorway, left to right, not up and down.

"Did you see who's here?" she said.

"No, I've been back here," I said.

"I know, but Robin Culver's here."

"Really?" I said.

Celebrities weren't that out of the question. Our supermarket was in New York City. But I knew Robin.

"I know Robin," I said.

"You do not. How?"

"We went to high school together. We weren't friends really but I knew her."

Sandra's eyes widened. "Are you going to say anything to her? You should go up and say hello."

"I don't know, Sandra. She doesn't care about me. She…"

"C'mon, right now. This will be fun. Go out and say hello to your friend from high school."

Sandra stepped up to the desk and lifted me up by the elbow. I have to admit, I was kind of pleased. It felt a little bit like being famous, fame by association. It would give everyone something to talk about. Which was nerve-wracking in a way – I didn't like people talking about me. That's why I liked the office tucked in the back of the market. But somehow, because Robin was famous, it made it OK, like criticism didn't hurt.

When I left the office, I could see people smiling, whispering to each other, looking in her direction. It was the kind of music that greeted her wherever she went.

I was standing at the registers. Sandra was back at her station. I heard her say, "Sally knows Robin Culver."

"She does?"

"She's going to talk to her."

I was getting nervous that something was expected of me. Like it was that chemistry report all over again. But I thought, I'm fifteen years older now. Things like this shouldn't matter anymore. I'm not the same person I was.

So I walked the aisles and found Robin in the juice aisle. She was standing there looking at the shelves and it was like I was in the wild and suddenly came across some rare animal. She looked great. She was wearing sunglasses as if to be inconspicuous. But she didn't really need to. They didn't disguise anything. But they made her look sort of aloof.

I think she had just gotten done exercising. She was wearing tight black bicycle-type pants. I don't know how a person could be that thin. Not *too* thin, perfectly thin. It was like having money and being successful had transformed her body, made her not completely human.

She was cradling a basket in one arm. There were only three items in the basket. I thought, she could afford to put anything in that basket. She could afford the entire store.

I walked up to her and I said, "Hi, Robin."

"Hi," she said, and looked back at the shelves. She had a sports drink, a jar of artichoke hearts, and some pita bread, that was it.

"It's me," I said. "Sally Cooper."

She looked up at me and raised her glasses above her eyes.

"Sally Cooper!" she said, very cheerily. "It's so great to see you." There was nothing in her voice. It was high-pitched and friendly-sounding, but empty.

"From high school," I added.

She studied me a little bit and her smile turned to a frown.

"Do you remember?" I asked, smaller.

"I'm sorry," she said, not smiling at all. "A lot of people say they went to high school with me. It was a long time ago."

"We did a chemistry report together."

"Like I said, I don't remember," she said curtly. "It was good to see you though."

With that she walked down the aisle away from me. She bought her things and was gone.

I was left standing in the juice aisle. I straightened up what she had been touching. She hadn't messed it up but it was something to do. I felt like crying. In fact, I did a little bit. I felt like all the products were watching me.

A few months later something happened. Her husband, Tim Griffith, was shot by a deranged celebrity stalker named Raymond Tompkins. He wanted to make an example of Tim Griffith, who he thought represented superficiality. That's what it said in his letter which was found in his apartment later on. Robin Culver's life was turned upside down. They were at a premiere and she watched her husband get shot. I work at a supermarket so I'm surrounded by the tabloids. This story was written about in some form for many, many weeks.

I thought about writing Raymond Tompkins. I don't know why exactly. He was misguided, but also I didn't like how everybody in the supermarket, how everybody everywhere, was talking about the shooting. Like it was as great a tragedy as the JFK assassination. I mean, please. I don't advocate anyone getting shot, but Tim Griffith was just an actor. "I feel so bad for them," they said. As if it was worse than something happening to their own family. These people making $8 an hour were distraught because some millionaires had some trouble.

So I wrote to Tompkins in prison. I said that I didn't condone what he had done but that I understood where he was coming from. Celebrities do get too much credit. They don't understand what it's like for regular people, even if they play them in the movies.

It didn't take too long, but I got a letter back. The letter came in an envelope stamped with the name of the prison. Funny, it was like getting a letter from a celebrity. How often do I get a letter from someone in the news, from anyone for that matter? I was nervous opening it. In fact, I didn't open it for a few minutes. I just stared at the envelope. I was sort of pleased with it and I didn't want to ruin that feeling by reading what he wrote to me. I didn't know the man. He was crazy, they said. Maybe he hated what I wrote to him. My heart couldn't take that. It was like I wrote a story and sent it to a publisher and I was waiting for acceptance or rejection. Of course, I was curious, so I opened the letter. Inside there were four pieces of notebook paper, cut neatly along the perforated edge, handwritten. His writing was easy enough to read.

Dear Sally, it started.

It was so great to hear from you. I get some hate mail, some love letters. Yours was one of the only ones that was in between. You addressed me like a person, not some kind of freak. So I liked it. What is it you do out there in the real world?

About what you wrote. Yeah, I've kind of come down from where I was. I was obsessed or possessed or both. Sometimes I feel bad about injuring a person. Maybe that's a cop-out. I'm glad he's not dead. I was more interested in making an example of an idea. I think I've done that much. I could have gone and shot the Hollywood sign, but that wouldn't have done any good. Maybe I should have set it on fire.

I'm glad you haven't gotten sucked into the news about this. It's all propaganda. Some guys here are afraid of me because of it. They don't know what the hell to make of me. The news is of course slanted entirely against me. What they don't know is that I've gotten in contact with people like you, good people. So how could it be entirely wrong?

I hope you'll stay in touch.

Ray Tompkins

We did stay in touch. I read that first letter four times through, right away. It was exciting, really one of the most exciting things I'd ever done. It was safe too because he was stuck in prison so he could never come after me. I was a little afraid. I never wrote that to him, but it was on my mind, at least at first. I wrote back:

I hope you're safe. The other inmates must feel weird that you tried to kill somebody who kind of belongs to everybody. Please take care of yourself.

You asked, so here goes: I work in a supermarket. A pretty dull job when you boil it down. I won't call it as bad as prison but I just go to work in a small, fluorescent-lit office, come home and sit in my apartment. Sometimes I read or watch TV. Then I go back again.

I felt bad about that letter. The part about TV. He hated TV and celebrities and all that so he might judge me for it. But he didn't say anything. He just wrote back that he liked my letter. And some stuff about what he was going through in the months before the attempted murder.

It was the brightest part of my life. I sailed through the workday. When I went to the supermarket, I'd feel as though

I were in love. Like I had this beautiful private world that no one knew about. I was really happy.

One letter, he asked for pictures. I had been expecting it, but it still threw me. Why shouldn't he want to know what I looked like? But also he was a lonely man in prison. And he might be picturing someone else. The magic could come out of it. Still though, it seemed unfair that I should see so many pictures of him – pictures from the trial, pictures from his childhood, pictures with his parents – and he shouldn't see a picture of me. I'll be honest too, I liked the idea of my picture keeping him company.

I took photos with a digital camera in my bathroom. I put up this nice tapestry I have – an Indian print – for a background, put on more make-up than I usually do, eyeliner, blush, and took a batch of pictures.

There aren't many good pictures of me because I am always blinking for the flash. I think part of me just doesn't want my picture taken. Four came out right. I always blink for flashes. It's a weakness or a compulsion.

He wrote back:

I loved the pictures So many people look like they're trying to look like somebody else. You look like exactly who you are. I don't know, timeless maybe. I think it's beautiful. I've taped up a picture in my cell.

One morning at the supermarket, I made a mistake. There was another manager at the market, named John, who was higher-up in the ranks and came in occasionally. He was nice enough. He sort of reminded me of myself, but a man. Not womanly, but he was twenty-five pounds overweight, balding, looked like he might have been decently attractive for a couple of years in his twenties but it faded quickly. He even asked me out once, but I said no because we worked so closely together. And he wasn't good enough. I don't know what it was about him. Too eager, maybe.

I told him I had been corresponding with Ray Tompkins. I just wanted to tell someone about it. At first, it was nice to have this kind of secret, but then I felt like telling someone.

"You know Ray Tompkins?" I said. We were in the fluorescent office, the two of us, which made the room a whole lot smaller. John was always self-conscious around me, always acting like we were touching.

"Who? Does he work here?" John asked.

"No, Ray Tompkins. The man who tried to kill Tim Griffith at that movie premiere. Around a year ago."

"Oh yeah, him. Nutcase. What about him?"

"We've been sending letters back and forth. He's actually a

pretty decent guy."

"I bet," he said derisively. "Why'd you want to do something like that?"

"I thought he seemed interesting."

"He's a murderer."

"He's not a murderer. Tim Griffith is OK. He's fine now."

John gave me this look.

I realized this was a mistake. I forgot that I would have to defend myself.

John was above me too; he was a more senior manager at the market. He was the liaison between corporate headquarters and all the markets in the region. It was a stupid mistake to tell him about it. Really stupid.

That night, I wrote to Ray about how I told my boss, but it would be a while before I got a response back. In the meantime, John recommended that I go into psychological counseling. The corporation had their own counselor.

"It's weird," John said.

"You don't understand," I said. "He's a good person. He just went through a bad phase."

"He's a lunatic and a criminal and it doesn't look very good for someone who works for this corporation in any capacity to be involved with him. You need to stop this correspondence."

"And what if I don't?" I said.

"If you don't," John said, "then I think we will have to look into terminating your employment with us."

Fuck him, I thought. And that's what I said, "Fuck you."

He looked shocked, a quick intake of breath, like I'd just slapped him.

"Sally, don't do this," he said.

"No, if I can't have some kind of extracurricular life, I don't want to work at this market anymore. It's like a prison."

"OK," he said. He did look regretful then, like he didn't really want to fire me, but he had to. He was a nice enough person. A robot, but a nice person. "We'll have to let you go."

"OK." I turned and walked out of the office quickly, as if to keep myself from having second thoughts, even though this was out of my control. I walked up to the registers kind of triumphantly. "I got fired," I said. I felt teary and sort-of high, like a Western stand-off where I might die, kind of confident and fearful at once.

I walked away before I could get a response. I wanted to be left with the image of their shocked, pitying looks, and my triumphant gait, probably more upright than I had been in years. Then I walked out of the supermarket, as if for the first time in my life.

Sally, Ray wrote, *I'm sorry that you lost your job. But fuck them. Now we can be together.*

LESSONS FROM ABOVE THE HOLE

Richard Price

I climbed the hill
To Understand
And have a talk
With the Brown Eyed Man

In a dark voice, gritty,
He said with a wink,
"Don't struggle so hard.
Take time to think.

The circle of Life
Don't travel that far.
Like a one-wheeled cart
You are, you were, you are.

Your braggadocio in the light
Turn silent whispers in the night.

Your calling card, your Nom De Plume,
But silent whispers inside the tomb.

The High, the Low – they all must go;
It's Nature's hungry ebb and flow.
Now breath in heavy truth's delight
And strike a match to make it right."

With no more dues abaft to pay
And not a single deuce to play,
No counterpoint, no Coup Fourrés,
The time was ripe to get away.

To stand upright, not bowed in shame.
To weather the storm, not take the blame.
No one has transcendent claim;
Out the end, we're all the same.

My business done,
Done what I can,
Upon the hill
With the Brown Eyed Man

From
IN ALL STATES A STRANGER
Russell DiNapoli

Sad to say, the author has taken a turn for the worse. He's staring emptily at a nearly drained bottle of cheap cognac perched atop a grimy stack of papers. Snatching up the bottle he downs another swig, gags and stares into space. By the looks of him, you'd think he was ruminating profoundly on something. But he is, in fact, not thinking at all. In a pretense of writing, he slides his hands from one end of the typewriter keyboard to the other. There is no paper in the carriage, which he manages with some difficulty to remediate. Like a German stormtrooper on the Russian front, he gazes into the infinite whiteness before him. Then tap tap tap in rapid fire. Word tracks appear. They trail off to nowhere. Hyperventilation shifts into a sonorous idle and suddenly he's gone… To Barcelona, reliving the first night he lay with Vicky beneath clean white sheets. Shouting can be heard outside their hotel window. It's 1939 and the Fascists are marching triumphantly in the streets, pummeling anyone not like themselves. In a cold sweat, he shivers fitfully. Vicky's arms gently reach for him and guide him inside her. It's all in your head, she whispers. He weeps, profoundly grateful.

He glances back at the blank sheet of paper with its hieroglyphic tread marks to nowhere. Tap tap tap. He follows the disarray of syllables, imagining he can bring them together somehow. He scans the horizon for a direction, and hears himself, who is not himself really, say, Go on, frame the picture. Sprinkle the words with cologne. Make them look sweet and sharp. Give it unity, logic, a purpose. Tap tap tap. That's the stuff. Linear movement. Line after line. Paragraph them. Big ones, small ones, some the length of a page or a chapter. Make it make sense. Don't write the same word twice in a sentence! Use a thesaurus. Forget about whether or not Dostoyevsky had one. Check the meaning of your words, and watch your spelling. That's what a bloody dictionary's for! Steer clear of run on sentences and dangling prepositions. Clean it up. Write with a critic's eye. Step back and evaluate. What's the theme? Is it fresh and innovative? Just look at the mess you've made! You've smeared that pristine white sheet of paper with offal again. The story's a total wreck. It doesn't hang together at all. There's not a significant thought anywhere. No meaning to be found. Get a grip. Start afresh. Call up your reserves. Line up the recruited words and march them down across another page!

Springing to his feet, he teeters like a buffalo that's just been shot. He drops and hits the floor, beside the scattered remains of the books he's been gluttoning himself on of late. His eyelids succumb to gravity. He sees himself driving along the road to Jativa as it winds around the northern edge of the Albufera. The great lake is separated from the Mediterranean by a zig-zagging frontier of pine trees and high-rises which, from where he sits, might as well be that as anything else… Come another day he'll write, it's all in the way you look at these things, and has little to do with how others see them. Reason assures me that nothing makes any real sense, anyway. That it all clears up in the eye of the beholder eventually. Or not.

Dear Reader,

The author's verbal incontinence only reflects his severely unstable condition. The reader may well be asking themself by now, Why go on? There's no point to all this. But make no mistake about it, potential genius in its primal stages is always a rather gaseous unintelligible mass. It requires, to say the least, perseverance and a great deal of nerve before acquiring a solid state, or the semblance thereof. Admittedly, though, it seems our candidate is down for the last count. The flat he occupies is a disaster zone. It reeks of BO, filthy teeth and boozy breath.

The odor of coitus lingers everywhere. The windows are shut and the curtains drawn. On the door a sign has been tacked bearing the only words our genius in the rough has written in ages: Let not the air within escape. At the moment, he and Maria Victoria are lying naked and dead to the world on a sheetless mattress soiled beyond repair. A gathering of cigarette burns and dried puddles of spilled wine proscribe the legibility of the writer's so-called manuscript. Funeral silence hovers over the setting. When a miracle occurs… . Tap tap tap. There in the penumbra sifting his way through the keyboard letters is the writer again. He's trying his best to hoist some order onto the rickety madness. He's telling us, in a surfeit of words, that a man—himself—has left his wife for another woman. Admittedly a run-of-the-mill tale, as old as the hills. What of it, one naturally asks? He swears on his life he's madly in love now with the latter as once he was with the former. Playing on the keys with his sticky fingers, he's trying to bring it together, to make it feel right, to give it some kind of narrative spin to warrant redemption. If anything, I can vouch for his mental instability and plead for the reader's mercy in judging him. He rants and raves, What have I done? Why am I doing this? Tears of rage erupt from his bloodshot eyes as he rips another sheet of paper from the carriage and sends it flying in my direction. I'm sorry for him. I pity the futility of the creative endeavors of those like him whom those in the know disdain. Poor wretch. No one will ever comprehend what he's trying to capture in words. Least of all himself. Without a reputable critic—say a Harvard or Oxford University professor with tenure—who'll risk their own prestige praising his literary merit he can't possibly expect readers to appreciate his emotional vagaries and see his work as anything but trite. Yet even plagued by this realization he continues to plug away at narrating the supposed significance of his self-inflicted plight. It is both the source of his profound unhappiness and the root of his transcendence. Truth be told, we're all attracted to a relentless fighter. The author's forthrightness arouses a pleasant sensation derived from pity. What is more, feeling sorry for him makes me feel superior, while at the same time I must acknowledge that his stupidity is, after all, a very human trait. What is particularly attractive about the author, though, is his obdurate insistence on what others more reasonably would interpret as a sentimental delusion. Against all reason he maintains that his love for María Victoria de las Mercedes is something special. God-like even. I must admit, notwithstanding the futility of it, his earnestness moves me. It is, to say the least, entertaining to follow out of morbid curiosity these demented Calibans through the thickets of their agonized souls. But alas, the ravings of a lunatic are but ephemerally interesting. A heartbeat or two longer and it becomes plain embarrassing to behold. Poor loser that he is. With the dramatic skill of a talented author, a titillating story might have unraveled of how two young lovers hitched a ride to Paris with a pair of Italian drug smugglers and the sundry adventures that evolved therein. But alas, amazing grace has abandoned him in the lurch. The muses just passed him by without ado, leaving him with a hackneyed story less the genius it would take to make it soar. For my part, it's time I withdrew my attention from his piteous pigheadedness and feasted my eyes on literarily worthier concerns.

Yours etc.

Vicky perused the sullied pages fastidiously. It was the first time I'd let anyone look through the tatters of this story. My thumping heart and a buzzing horsefly were the only sounds in the room. I was sweating profusely, trying to maintain a semblance of nonchalance for what seemed like an eternity. When at last she sighed and screwed up her eyes. I stood there waiting like a condemned prisoner before a firing squad. She laid into me. Frankly, this 'beyond me' lingo is a bunch of crap! You need to have more faith in yourself and your writing. Forget about trying to be understood. No matter what you say or how you say it, people will only interpret it as they see fit.

There's nothing you can do about it. In the end it's the risks you take that make the thing worth reading.

....

In this garden baptised Valencia, what the Romans called Valentina Edetanorum—the city of the brave—and the Muslims Balansiya—the apotheosis of beauty—the effusive odor of shit fertilizes rejuvenation, contrasting with the pervasive scent of orange blossoms that bears florescence to lustier senses. It is where I linger now with the local down and outs like myself prowling like stray dogs the ever dwindling remains of the *huerta valenciana.* I'm a citizen for the moment of the fertile fields of this Mediterranean Mesopotamia. But I know come one morning I'll have left it all behind the way I had The Big Apple that bore me and the City of Angels that branded my hide. I suspect that lives lived in time, like stories and poems, are never completed, but abandoned in place. We're Extranjeros en Todos los Estados, I assure myself in my new-found language. In all states a stranger, we endure like a perennial harvest moon over the solitude of our being.

VALENCIA, 1979

MY SOUL TORN APART

MK Malther

Translation from the Spanish by Edgar Barrios

I didn't know who you were, couldn't recognize you
Couldn't recognize those eyes that one day looked at me with love
Or so I thought
How was it possible that now, they would look at me with such hatred?

But yes it was you, the same, the father of my children
Beating me down, kicking my stomach and my face

Not only my body, breaking my soul apart
How was it possible that everything has changed so fast?
How was it possible that you didn't care about anything?
You left me lying on the cold floor as usual
I tried to escape, but there was no way out
I tried to run away but you caught me again

You hit me again and I wondered again
Where was the kind man that I fell in love with?
The one that promised me everything would be alright

Now was treating me like rubbish
Treating me like a stranger

You didn't care about our kids, you didn't care about anything
You kept on hurting me, it hurt like hell
It hurt, my soul was torn apart
Broken in a million pieces

But time is wise, time made me stronger
Life made me stronger and i managed to escape, I managed to leave you
I manage to run away, I managed to bury you

Now, finally you don't mean anything to me, you're simply the stranger I met 30 years ago
Now I'm finally happy and can live in peace.

INFINITE SADNESS FOR PABLITO

MK Malther

Translation from the Spanish by Edgar Barrios

Always in my mind your bleak smile
Always in my brain your little absent eyes
Your gelid little hands, your cold and empty body
Where has your soul gone?

I arrived late, soon they were waiting for you already
I arrived late, because you were leaving

I couldn't even hear your crying
I couldn't even touch your hand
They took you away immediately
But they couldn't take you away from my mind

I arrived late, couldn't find you
I arrived late, your time was coming

I sent some screams to heaven, but nobody heard
I sent some screams to heaven, but it was refused
My good friend was already there

My good friend, she was waiting for you

I arrived late, because she is punctual
I arrived late, and I felt like being stabbed

It doesn't matter how long it is
It doesn't matter how far we've been sent
You will always be my angel on my sleeplessness
And I will be the mother that still loves you in her dreams.

DESTROY TO EXIST

Savanna Evans

Another girl with her pants down

Security running to the centre
Of a crowd of ID
2 am
From the tower it's a current in the sea
The island of dancers
In the crowd she feels hands
Unnumbered
Everywhere
"WANTED TITS + ACID"

'Lunatic fringe'
'Few bad apples' afterwards

I have my shirt off because this is my body
of '69
Is the free for all since the 90s

And we still argue over this

He gripped cardboard that read
"Show us ur tits" and grinned

He can pass out and wake up with his
Pants buttoned
She wakes ups
As another girl with her pants down.

Woodstock thirty years apart

They Exist to Destroy

Only her sleeve in the security's fist

Bullets contained
'Like unleashing a champagne cork'

'PEOPLE DEMAND REMOVAL…' on
bedsheets

He's the bridge between them
In a crowd of ID

the camera battery dies
the recording cuts - so does the camera flash

They've said: 'Let's take her pants off'

She feels hands
Unnumbered
Front and back

Dropped in the lap of their woman
Her black niqab

'ANIMALS' on paper

A decade from Woodstock '99

We can say your name, Laura Logan.

ANOREXIA IN BROOKLYN

Alice Hlidkova

I sliced a scallop in half with a sharp knife, feeling hunger claw at my stomach. Eighteen calories, I noted. My eyes flicked over to John as he dipped apple wedges into peanut butter, his version of a meal.

"How many scallops do you want?" I kissed my boyfriend on the cheek.

"Just three," he whispered, clutching his stomach. "I can't handle more than that." He shifted against the pillow, nudging aside the bedcovers.

"Is your stomach bothering you again?" I moved closer to the bed and leaned down, resting my ear against his abdomen. A soft rumble echoed from deep inside. I stood up and encircled his neck with my arms. His eyes followed the lines of my elbows, outlining the bones under my skin.

"You're getting stronger," he tried to smile. "But are you happy?" His words stung, but I buried them and returned to the kitchen.

Our apartment was a cozy studio on Bergen Street in Brooklyn, with soft lighting that added to its charm. Just around the corner, the fish shop's window glistened with ice showcasing fresh catches: salmon, sardines, and octopus. Beside it, the butcher's counter displayed rich marbled steaks, thick pork chops, and neatly tied roasts.

I placed half a scallop in the pan, then three more, calculating quickly: eighteen for me, one hundred and eight for him. One tablespoon of olive oil, one hundred twenty. We need to split that. While opening the fridge for the yogurt, my mind raced with numbers—fifty-nine calories a cup, about three per tablespoon. I needed just two. The scallops sizzled, reminding me to flip them before they burned.

"Have you seen the doctor this week?" John's voice broke through my focus.

"Yeah," I said, tallying up my calculations.

"What did he say?" he pressed, looking concerned.

I clenched my fists and turned sharply to face him, my patience fraying like the edge of a well-worn cloth. "Baby, I'm trying to focus here."

"Sorry," he muttered.

"I don't want to burn the scallops."

John sauntered into the kitchen, planting a kiss on my neck. "Can I help?"

"No, just rushing—class starts in an hour," I replied, glancing at the scallops. He nudged one, slicing it in half.

"Now there are two halves," he grinned. "Two halves make a whole."

"Cute," I smiled briefly, then turned back to the stove. The oil in the pan snapped, spitting droplets that sizzled. The smell of burning scallops filled the room. I glanced at John, hoping he hadn't noticed. He was digging at his teeth with his nail. Beside him, a magazine lay on the floor, its pages slightly curled from the heat.

I placed two and a half scallops on his plate and set it in his lap. Grabbing a sweatshirt, I picked up my yoga mat. "Baby, I have to go, or I'll be late," I said, urgency in my voice.

"You won't eat?" he asked, looking at the plate.

I forced a smile and took a scallop from the plate. "See? I ate," I replied as I hurried out the door. Only thirty-six calories, I thought. Fifty with the oil?

As I walked six streets down, the air was filled with the scents of hazelnut and cardamom from a nearby coffee roaster. The enticing aroma drew me inside. There, I observed the women—thin, with long legs and tasseled hair, leaning over their cups. Like them, I stood holding my coffee, all of us artworks of New York City.

In this city where every moment was a stage, I caught my reflection in the window. The realization hit me: we were all striving to be seen and validated in a race marked by fleeting glances and superficial praise. Was this pursuit of perfection worth the struggle? Wouldn't you question the same?

I took a sip of coffee, burning my tongue, and walked into the studio. Tying my shirt into a knot, I checked my hips in the mirror, tied my shirt into a knot, and sucked in my stomach; flat today, my precious. I pulled up my yoga pants and unrolled my mat between two brunettes twirling their ponies. These women, so beautiful and perfectly sculpted, seemed like they stepped off the runway at New York Fashion Week. Why couldn't I be like them? We stood on our mats and lifted our arms. As I stretched, my ribs jutted out, stark against my skin. I glanced sideways at the brunettes, their hip bones gracefully jutting out, legs extending like marble columns. My reflection felt softer, stubborn curves refusing to blend into the same sleek lines.

Yoga practice in Brooklyn was a kaleidoscope of women wrapped in spandex of all colors, a blend of thin and heavyset bodies. New York City, like LA and Miami, had the most gorgeous women, their skin tones sparkling, lashes thick as spider legs. Even new moms, without makeup, managed to show up in shape, juggling life with a newborn. Women from all walks of life with big dreams, bank accounts, full or nearly empty, and with that came talent, hungry boys for money and the prize between their legs. Whether to keep the men or attract them, yoga women kept shape, their bodies, and prime real estate.

I knew the market I was in, and I wasn't stupid. A trifecta one might call a unicorn outperformed the rest—beautiful, smart, ambitious. To compete, I shaved the fat, hustled, crashed parties, and blacked out. At 110 pounds, and naturally small-boned, I watched my weight like my mother, twenty pounds heavier than me. "Three pounds more; I need to do something about it," she'd say, opting for a walk to the park over pastries. Her reward: a glass of wine before sunset, and a handful of chips. Something small, gluten-free. She liked her sweets, sharing croissants with the little girl she babysat. Baking she reserved for her husband; my stepfather loved her cakes and breads, mixed with zucchini or carrots. I wondered whether she added the vegetables to feel better about herself, the wife and mother administering healthy carbs, as a substitute for more butter and sugar.

Every holiday meal was a silent contest of indulgence and restraint, followed by the inevitable guilt of eating too much and too late. My mother, never eating past five, kept her nose close to her plate—a habit she'd developed as a child under communism.

I picked at the breaded fish skin, fried in sunflower oil, my stomach tightening with every bite. My stepfather, a slow eater, meticulously picked at the bones, savoring each morsel. Often, I escaped to the bathroom before washing the dishes, lifting my shirt to inspect my stomach in the mirror, convinced I saw a bulge.

I wished for a device that could weigh my stomach alone, to confirm my fears. Tracking calories was often impossible because I wasn't making the meals, and Mom's complex potato salad had too many ingredients to count. The family tradition of carp fish for Christmas was particularly stressful. Just like my boyfriend, my stomach twisted into knots at the thought. If we had it our way, we'd mark the calendar date with a big, fat "X."

At my father's house in the country where I was born, Czechoslovakia, meat and potatoes dominated most meals. Vegetables were rare, limited to four options: tomato, cauliflower, cucumber, and bell peppers. I couldn't count calories either, as I didn't prepare the meals.

My favorite moments were the rare trips to get ice cream with my dad, where I could scrutinize the labels, or when we ate salted crackers by the TV. Each cracker was easy to count, and my dad, a binge eater, became my target for scolding.

"Dad, you don't need to eat another pack," I'd say, watching him reach for more.

"Haven't you already had a bottle of wine? Do you need another?" I'd ask, my voice edged with concern.

He would laugh, a carefree sound that made my worries seem insignificant. "A bottle is nothing. Besides, wine is healthy," he'd say, waving off my concerns. His girlfriend, a daughter of a winemaker, would nod in agreement, her smile deep and wise, like she held some ancient secret.

In winter, Dad's belly would grow, gaining 10-20 kilos. But come spring, he'd tackle the slopes of Italy and Austria on his bike, shedding the weight with a determination that seemed almost heroic. I'd watch him, marveling at how easily he could transform, while I struggled to maintain control over every bite.

I never thought I had an issue with food because no one in the family spoke about their problems. We lived normal lives with bad habits, oscillating between weight gain and loss, guilt and shame. Eating disorders like anorexia are mental health conditions affecting not just young, affluent, pretty white girls but also people with thick skin and boys. One in every three anorexia cases in America is a young boy.

Every time I eat scallops, I think of Brooklyn. I no longer want to slice them in two. I want to eat several, which I do alone. Yet, I still slice bananas in half, break cookies into pieces, crush nuts, and eat from smaller bowls. After eating, my stomach swelled uncomfortably, and my mind drifted into a haze, every thought heavy and syrupy, my limbs sluggish as though wading through molasses. Ulcers and intestinal scars now plague me, and every meal feels like knives cutting my guts. But as I placed the last piece of scallop in my mouth, the taste mingling with a bittersweet realization, I felt a sliver of hope. For the first time, acknowledging the problem felt like a tiny, trembling step toward something better.

CINNAMON TEA

Edgar Barrios

Yeah you matter

No I really mean it,

Look at you

With your degrees and your social connections

Pretty good for a poorly domesticated monkey now with anxiety!

thousand bodies dying together

In my dreams

Kor's floating head

A beheaded leopard in NY

A hot cup of apple cinnamon tea

The sunset

Showering my head

A night full of dead stars

Million years ago they were just like me

Inside,

there is no time

My galaxy is empty

Eroded

Trees emerge from the ground

Trying to touch me

Trying to reach me

Trying to live

Dumb muthafucking trees they will never know that

Fire makes me cry

Is it an instant or a second?

An eternity

What is this?

Can't tell

Vanilla textures

Beer-flavored mist

Withered soul but

I got a couple of VIP tickets

To tame the beast

Masturbate this melancholic feeling

The beast isn't alone

He told me

Tell my new lover my body is a secret garden

Even though we know is a dirty public park

A mosquito buzzing in my paranoid ears

The heat of times

Spontaneous human combustion

Do you want me to be proud this month? Or you just want
to sell some trendy shit to me?
I see
I'll tell you all your favorite catchphrases
Yes daddy
To satisfy all your unresolved trauma
Is this the universe experiencing itself?
Or are we merely reduced to penetrating bodies and
Manipulating people that love you

Cuz I thought I had been Raining in red galaxies for a while

Dissonance
I'm not very eloquent
My character is a zombie inside a zombie
bubble gum zombies
Stain the art
Gray almost everywhere
Atoms to dissolve my riot
Plastic to cover my apathy
Clandestine cemeteries in which the fear of being afraid ends
Bastardize your eternal beauty
By seeing yourself only as on object of desire
I don't want to hear your grandma stories

Let's get down to business he said

Skipped a couple of songs

The fire won't stop burning

And this tropical love keeps boiling under my ribs

Being is a catastrophe

The unbearable lightness of being gay

Ghost kid, ghost teen,

Two-headed snake

Sugar fucking Aphrodite

I can't conceive why you can't see all my blackness and all my darkness

Chips and microchips

Bionic mosquitos

Entertainment for everyone

I thought I wasn't gonna break all my promises

My beautiful prince rests in his palace

My heart has jumped off the roof

And this yellow demon won't let me die in peace.

EL INCIENSO (REQUIEM)

Edgar Barrios

El Incienso is a bridge that connects the violent city of Guatemala; this bridge has been the hotspot for suicidal souls in my hometown since I have recollection of things: people who have been brokenhearted, lost their faith, or have reached the end of the spiral. This poem is dedicated to all those brave ones.

Forgive me father for what I'm about to do he said
Got closer to the edge of the bridge
wind running beneath his trembling feet
Distant voices from people yelling and begging him to come down
Echoes buzzing, white noise in his paranoid ears

We shouldn't make love anymore
We shouldn't bastardize this grandiose ecstasy with cheap modern fvcking relationships
We are all afraid of being afraid
Melting gold medals to decorate my ego
I don't belong anywhere, Halluci-nations of a rat

Don't ever make love again
The joy of watching it burn
Cuz tell me if not, people that were supposed to love you more have hurt you the most
We shouldn't make love anymore
We should tear it apart
Dismantle it
Dissect it
Love is dead but your heart's not bleeding
It is all an illusion,
That separate us from other mammals
Narcissistic shallow little people
The audacity to call our own destruction progress

Don't ever make love again
Fold it, break it in half
and let the little rabbits of your despair carry the corpse to its funeral
One day you´ll be space dust and you will fingerfuck the center of the universe
And we will rain forever over cherry trees
One day you will meet your own mirror and save yourself

I am
A hurricane in mute, the private thunder
This galloping apocalypse
A quiet torment
Small hands of a broken poet
I am the storm after the storm
that millisecond inside my brain
And we all jump sometimes

I want air that has never been breathed
Eternal roses full of mosquitos
Eternal roses full of pain

ignorant observer

Uliana (Jay) Tarnopolska

barely standing up
she's holding on to the handrail
and whenever the train abruptly stops
she flinches
and her overgrown and half broken nails
clink against the metal
i'm standing across to her
and feel like a hypocrite
with my little backpack and script in hand
with my little evening prayer
and dreams of becoming a poet
barely standing up
on her tall and uncomfortable heels
that got dirty in the morning rain
she looks older than she is
in her tall and uncomfortable heels
she'd look taller than she is
if she didn't hunch her back

if she wasn't being violently pierced
with a gaze of ignorant observers
she has semen in her hair
and blood on her lower lip
there is no pride to her stance
she's just trying to hold on to the handrail
she is a sister to a little girl
she too has been her mother's little girl
she too has been a little girl once
i look at her, studying her every detail,
watching her every move
ashamed, ashamed, ashamed
I turn away. I am a coward.
i get home and turn off my phone
i get undressed and stand under the water
i smoke on my balcony
i build a cocoon around me
and curl up there, quietly
without a sound
just waiting for my consciousness to slip away somewhere
My chosen blindness
My phone buzzing from
the abundance of
party dresses and dancing and cake

I am a coward
Every morning i pass by the campus
the lawn is covered in tents
i imagine this same lawn
covered in bloody corpses
lifeless bodies on the ground
surrounded by chirping unsuspecting birds
starving dogs eating them
I wish I was a bird too
I wish I was a little girl
I wish I didn't know the value of a human life
I am a coward
But there was love, of course there was
A mother is holding a baby close to her chest
she is singing, quietly, just for him
she is singing a lullaby
blood runs down her legs
she's sitting on the ruins of her home
the baby sleeps soundly
she's singing with a tremble in her voice
she sings with her voice
I am too afraid to raise mine
I am a coward
I am a coward with a phone in hand

a phone that talks to me
tells me what to wear in the morning
and what to eat
tells me grief is temporary
sending thoughts and prayers via email
i walk down the street
and hide my eyes from strangers
that are ready to tear me apart
at any given moment
steal and violate
my precious feeling of safety
I'd like to be that person to hold these thoughts to light and
not even flinch
but it makes me shiver
just to see their odd shapes
reveal themselves under the moonlight
And yet I hold it close to my body,
as if my fragile human flesh can save it
It's not real
None of it is real
I'm a coward
I'm pushing through the riot crowd
working my elbows
somewhere knee deep in a

guilty anxious dream
i get kicked off my feet
by some primal fear.
I want to do it anyway
i'm stumbling somewhere around the corners
kick me out
let me in
make me feel like i'm doing something
anything
none of it matters, i'm weak
i fall to the floor and scrape my knees
they pin me to the floor
i feel a gun hit the back of my throat

a child is born in the middle of an abandoned hospital
sirens wail and red lights flicker
a mother is holding
her baby close to her chest
her little girl
warm and screaming
breathing in dusty air
a little breathing body, alive
anemone the gentle flower of spring
blossoms in the middle of a minefield
lovers make love for the last time

before they step into the uncertainty
they hold each other's faces
and promise to come home
caress each other's faces with their thumbs
hide their tears behind the smiles
and pray to whatever god is willing to listen
till death do them apart
"I love you, you hear me?"
she shouts on top of her lungs
louder than the atomic explosion
"I love you"
the girl from the metro
falls asleep without washing
her makeup off
holding a rabbit plush toy
greying with time
She sleeps on her side
just like she did when she was a child
I close my eyes shut
I put my earplugs in
This isn't happening
I could swallow a bullet
and rip into two
each part to hear each side

spill blood on the sand
to turn into anemones
or I could build a pillow castle
for me to hide
and turn away my gaze
like there's noone to sing a lullaby to.

fortune cookies

Uliana (Jay) Tarnopolska

1

when i packed my things
shoved my sentences in the bag
and swallowed my question marks
i looked back one last time
trying to remember his place
down to the very last detail
an open bag of chips
ashes on the bed sheets
a dead houseplant.
it was a little christmas tree
i got it for him as a gift
he didn't understand
what it meant
evergreen and shiny
then, christmas passed
and the little tree died neglected
i noticed it in a while

when things started to fall apart
we were sitting
on the opposite sides of his bed
when i looked at his drying branches
at his crumbling soil
i think i cried
i said "why do you keep
it's corpse in your room?"
he shrugged and stared down
"i'd feel sad throwing it out"
he promised to put it away
but he never did
i wanted to throw it to his face
or break it somehow
stomp on the pot shards

II

must have been a metaphor.
or a symbol, for sure
it's what i live by
fortune cookies
and star constellations
meteor showers
tea leaves on the bottom of my cup.
things in his house talked to me

a broken doorknob, a smashed bug
juxtapositions and alliterations
the unsaid, implied
in between pauses of
ends and beginnings
yet clear to me
he liked my nihilism, i liked his smile
transparent and fit like a shoe
a collarbone designed
specifically to fit my chin
beloved lines reread a million times
repeated like a prayer
unlike you... you must be
something from the bible, perhaps
or some kind of nightly vision
smiling subtly as you watch
me make the same mistakes
in the middle of the stage
stumble on my words
forget my lines, trip and fall.
or maybe just human, painfully
yearning to be known, too
i wish i could scream
and rip my hair out in frustration

of not seeing the smoke from your lips
form a regular rhyme scheme
a b a b, c d c d
i wish you could take me to your house
so i could whisper questions
to your kitchenware and pillowcase
about your dialect
i wish i could get straightforward answers
a b a b c d c fucking d
wish i could get under your skin somehow
listen to your heart beat in morse code
wish i could bite through you
solve you like a crossword
put my trembling mouth to your wounds
get to your core
because there is simply no other way
for me to read you.
but i could never have you,
not for myself, i could never keep you
caged away to admire
no, i want you
like one animal wants another
mumbling my stream of consciousness
intoxicated into your ear

with the faith of a devotee
and the mistrust of a sinner
running my fingers through your pages
like it's my last air.
I am waiting in front of a Chinese takeout
for another reason to tear my soul apart
inside a promotional fortune cookie
given to me for buying a meal and a soda
you're sitting in front of me
with crumbs on your sundress
with blood and organs inside your body
you read the prophecy and roll your eyes
i grow inpatient like i always do
and i don't want to know what the future holds
so dance with me.
dance while in my memory
you still have legs, arms and teeth
dance with me before the sun rises
before we're told we must make sense of this
dance before we get sober
dance before it gets vulgar to not ask questions
before we have to go live our lives
and forget we were ever half in love
for almost two whole weeks

before you leave me confused
and wanting more
than dead houseplants
smashed bugs and familiar collarbones
maybe because it's not a metaphor
nor a symbol
there are no implied answers
to the not-so-rhetorical questions
of whether this is almost romance
or simply a pure form of awe
or something without a name at all
maybe i am completely defenceless
in front of someone so human
and being perceived as one.
maybe you were never meant to stay
just collide and explode like a firework
you shook me awake
and made me spring new leaves
maybe I was never meant
neither for you nor for him
maybe prophets lied,
maybe tea leaves were swallowed unread
constellations were airplanes,
and all fortune cookies said the same thing

sweet nihilist

Uliana (Jay) Tarnopolska

july 2023

we smoked on his rooftop that summer
what a perfect rooftop for laying down
what a perfect rooftop for
wondering what could've been
side by side floating up the starry sky
but as you pass me my poison of choice
i couldn't face you
the way i still can't face you
uncomprehendable to the rest
then we struggled down the stairs,
all five of us,
and they were giggling like idiots
so loud, i was scared the cops will come
i couldn't hush them
he kept hitting his friend's shoulder
oblivious and happy and young
he must have forgotten i was there at all

i didn't blame him for it
it was so dark, i could forget myself too
but you, were you watching me?
because you found my fingers somehow
i grabbed your arm, then let go
then, i went down into his room
i told him about what we talked about
he just shrugged and said
it probably doesn't matter
he said something funny, then
i felt his flesh rise, as he reached
for my hips, bringing them closer
he felt my mouth and ribs
and i bent to him like grass in the wind

April 2024

spring nights are still too cold for me
i was pressing to you, freezing in the wind
like a trembling leaf
full of hope you could make me feel warm
i've been watching you smile at a wall
afraid to reach your fingers or lips
i sit in front of you
and watch you break me slowly
with piercing words of nihilism

we snuck into my kitchen
we just happened to
be drunk on a saturday night
and sit in complete silence
no reason why you took the last train
i guess it just happened to be the last
i felt like i was just kiss away
from baring my soul to you, but
none of this is for anything and none of this
will lead to anything more or anything else
and i'm not sure why
but that night i could feel tears in my throat
i also felt so angry
maybe i felt angry because you were right?
when i sat half drunk half in love
right in front of you i wanted to laugh
yes you were right
nothing matters,
existence is meaningless
and moreover bleak
bleak like staring into the ceiling
like feeling him panting on top of you
asking yourself repetitive questions
kissing any lips that make you feel alive

for a few quick passing moments
that's what it must feel like, to kiss me.

October 2023

I scratch the dog behind the ear
with the one hand free from shopping bags
i scrub and clean out the junk
behind the kettle and coffee machine
then open a window
to let the air in and smoke
every boy that doesn't believe in fate
needs a lover to show him it's colors
every man that never felt a mother's love
needs a gentle hand to caress his face
every hopeless soul
needs a dancer in the rain, a savior
someone to clean their counters
and somehow i don't blame him at all
all he needs is a little care
someone to show him it all matters
someone to take a blank canvas
and paint a fresh new meaning.

April 2024

I wish I could kiss the nihilism out of you

but my hand falls flat on the table
without reaching the top of your tired head
I am no savior, not anymore
but at this moment, how i wish i was
how i wish i could grab your arm
and take you far away from this place
how i wish i could show you your soul
make you believe in God or
anything else, you choose
and promise you'll feel alright again
But i can't promise you anything
because when I talk to God
he doesn't always answer me
I danced in the rain
i ran fingers through my hair
and smiled like i know something
i put on this show so many times
my legs are tired and cold
so i stand still, looking up at the water
falling in my face
meaningless and endless
i don't want to save you
i only want to ask you to say for the night
we could hold onto each other,

legs intertwined on my couch.
please don't be cold
please don't look away
I cling on to your lips
for the very last time
before you take the very last train
before i melt and soak
into the other side of my door
left alone face to face
with a yearning for a meaning.

AN ASTRONAUT'S FATE

Robin Souls (IG: @robin.souls)

When I was a kid I wanted to become great things when I grew up. Great things like a scientist, an inventor or even an astronaut! I guess now it shows off that I didn't become any of those…

Years were passing, as time is merciless. A merciless bitch we've been always struggling with.
I've spent many years of my life wondering what was I going to end up becoming but I'm not actually able to know entirely how events will happen, and neither do you.
Anything could happen.

That's how one day, I was looking into my own sky, wondering why it wasn't as bright and beautiful as I'd like it to be and other ones seemed to be.

And suddenly, I noticed a tiny and slightly brighter light in the distance. A spark of light that, somehow, awakened a dream of mine, long time lost.
The dream of becoming an astronaut.

So I started to assemble all the parts of my old, rusty ship, back then small and tight enough just for me to fit in and which has never been used before.
Already suited, seated in the cockpit.
Engines on. Destination set.

Are you sure you want to set this destination? — Yes.
It will probably be dangerous. There may be several meteor fields on the way, solar storm too. Are you really sure? — Yes.
Ship's getting ready to take off. The engines are already heating and I feel really nervous.

Then a flickering countdown and a message appeared on my screen.
- YOU HAVE A MINUTE TO CHANGE YOUR MIND AND ABORT THE MISSION -

My heart's never beat faster. Half a minute left for me to retract. Time's never felt so slow.

That's the moment I took to think about the actions and consequences that brought me to that determining moment and the many more that will come after. Thoughts were flying in my head like crazy little birds about to swell up and explode.

Ship's shaking. 4, 3, 2…1
Taking off.

Without realizing it, I was already crossing the atmosphere, as fast as a dart going straight into its target. I closed my eyes when I was about to cross the very last layer of the Earth, then opened them, and then, there was that extensive, dark, but also amazing space in which I was hoping all the things I did to get there were not in vain.

In less time than I realized, I was finally getting to my destination.
I was so close to the center of a newly discovered dimension with a sun, brighter than I could imagine.
About to pull the break and wanting to stay still and observing that astonishing, incredible, giant light at the same time the emergency lights started to flash so hard I could barely see. The ship's shaking violently, it can't stop now, there's no turning

back. Breaks are no longer useful. Heat's increasing, Trespassing the limits.

CRITICAL ERROR!
CRITICAL ERROR!

I was grabbing the controller so hard I kinda felt like it was melting. Then the back of the ship detached. One wing, the other one… and then, a liberating thought came across my mind.

I released the controller and opened my eyes to see during my last seconds of life the grandeur and beauty of that brilliant sun that ended up disintegrating my ship, with the greatest and most sincere of my smiles.

How many seconds have past? Am I dead yet?
My body's still here… But I collapsed into the sun! I don't understand…
I looked at myself. No. I'M REBORN! I WAS SHINING!
Shining and spreading in thousands of small shining fractals.
Have I become into a star?
Then I realized: No. I already was.

Now I'm also in someone's sky too and if events couldn't have happened that way, maybe I won't be there for that someone to look upon.

So there I was, becoming stardust and unveiling my own, true form as a whole new system, a new constellation, a new universe. Accepting myself for what I am and becoming one with all, shining so bright I could burn to ashes all of my fears and insecurities, but not to get totally rid of them, as they are part of what I am now. And I've learnt to be thankful to them. To my errors and my successes.

Old me might be dead now, or at least part of it, but I'm actually grateful for myself, for having the right people beside me, and for having the courage to jump into the void. To be the one who looks back at it, with a welcoming attitude for all the things yet to come in that beautiful universe I'm now part of, for the rest of my own eternity.

AN ARGUMENT BETWEEN AN ELIZABETHAN CONSPIRACY THEORIST AND HIS ESTRANGED FRIEND

Raymond Goslitski

My dearest Will, how dost thou, my old friend?
It's been at least a year and four score days
Since we both did go our separate ways,
And our last eve of discourse reached its end.

Good morrow Edward, hath it been so long?
I feel that it was only yesterday
That thou informèd me the queen was stray,
And plotting with that nefarious Spanish throng!

By my troth, dear Will, I met a man
Twixt Aldwych and the Strand last Ethelstide
In the privy of the Cross Keys Inn Bankside

Who proves the plague a wicked Spanish plan!

Nay verily Edward, I cannot abide
Plague deniers weakening my dear land!
Thou need'st a spanking by a noble hand
Thy nether regions brutally to chide!

But didst thou know they contaminate the sea
By fitting galleons with a noxious matter
To perpetuate those white streams in the water
Foam trails, as they be known (twixt you and me).

Thou needest right away an understanding:
Each and every month when moon is dark,
Spanish ships let soldiers disembark,
To fabricate these shady lunar landings!

Edward, noble cuz, thou art a fool
Wherefore dost thou gather such deceits?
I fear thou guilelessly take heed of cheats
Hast thou forsaken what thou learned at school?

The punishment for friends they label traitors;
They put men in the Thames all bound and tied,

Through a door that drowns by rising tide
These shameless scoundrels dubbed the Watergaters.

The wife of Robert, Earl of Ardingly
Did in a tunnel meet a gruesome killer
They said her carriage hit a central pillar,
We want to know: how did the Lady die?

John Lynman, the jolly ferryman, you know?
Did disappear attending to a call
From seven blackguards on the Galley wall
Whither did that merry Lynman row?

Moreover, Will, my spirit be no calmer,
The giant ploughman near to Southwark Road
Is selling faulty barley by the load
Scoundrels hawking seed for that Big Farmer.

They tell us that our language is a sop
To shifting vowels and consonants in change.
That kern be corn and gern we now call grain!
My lips reject phonetically modified crops!

Gadzooks, dear Ed, hast thou gone mad, perchance?
Thine witterings are cumbersome at best!
But shouldst thou leave, thine frame of mind to rest,
A change of climate would thine mood enhance.

Tush and fie, my kinsman, I bide well!
Methinks 'tis thee who seeth only fairies!
Hie thyself to Scott's Apothecary,
He's a lazy runt, but doth that sleeper sell!

Beware, though, for imposters do not lack.
Deceivers one and all, and how they flourish!
Ne'er do those physicians truly nourish,
Tarry ere thou cross those men in black!

Tom and Freddy Tower, you perhaps
Remember, sweating sickness sufferers, they.
In September on the eleventh day
Did those ill-fated Tower twins collapse.

I tell thee, this be no coincidence,
The physician drawing blood their death hath wrought,
Their lives were rendered in a flash to nought.
Thou art anti-leech if thou hast sense!

Do not at Aldgate for physicians look;
They cut off Henry's hand to treat for shock
And threw him on the beach near Deptford Dock
And since that day he hath a sandy hook

Prithee Will, thou think'st I would thee woe?
How these knaves do hover overhead!
They look down on us while we lie in bed,
And make believe I consider you a foe!

Edward, I must urgently move on,
But it was interesting to hear thy mind.
I beseech thee leave it all behind
Adieu, dear friend, I shall seek you anon!

THE BALLAD OF THE OFFENSIVE NATIONAL STEREOTYPE

Raymond Goslitski

I'm with friends on a terrace in a Valencian bar;
There's a bloke playing techno in his battered old car.
It's busy right now but he's managed to fit
His Nissan Micra in two spaces but he gives not a shit.

The family of ten on the table behind
Take turns to scream answers, often three at a time.
I'm finding it hard not to shout to be heard,
My companion picks up every third or fourth word.

There's a chain smoking lady and her gnarled old friend
Blowing foul, rancid chemicals from her position upwind.
To my left there's a tablet being watched by some kids
Volume on full as they flick through the vids.

And the father is making a private phone call:
His schedule tomorrow everyone knows it all.
And although this might seem quite contentious to some,
The self-conscious Spaniard is as rare as they come.

It's like finding a German in a comedy club
Or an Irishman who's never entered a pub.
A modest Parisian, a trilingual Brit,
These oxymoronic descriptions don't fit!

It's like Australian and stylish, or hairless and Greek,
Or Swiss and good-natured – wow, that sounds like a freak!
Like an Anglophile Scot… actually an Anglophile anyone…
Like a brown sunburned Scot neither angry nor sweaty,
Or an Italian who consciously cuts their spaghetti!

It's like meeting a Swede who does not seem so weird,
Even finding an Afghan not sporting a beard.
American tourists who know where they are
Or Sicilians driving an immaculate car.

Meek, humble Austrians and talkative Finns,
Alabamans not married to their next-of-kin;
Californians who've learned how to critically think,
Dutchmen who offer to pay for your drink,

Jean-Claude Van Damme or Jacques Brel, so that's two
Rubens, Magritte, Hergé, to name a few…
Audrey Hepburn, Eddy Merckx, Django Reinhardt,
I know more famous Belgians than self-conscious Spaniards!

Considerate Portuguese silent at night,
Kind Russian tourists well-bred and polite,
Hygienic teenagers obsessed not with fitness,
A rational statement from a Jehovah's Witness.

An LA pedestrian, a Qatari nun,
Texans who have never fired a gun,
A Londoner who earns enough to live there,
A Republican signed up to Obamacare.

A self-conscious Spaniard is uncommon indeed,
Like a Merc driver travelling at appropriate speed,
Like a plumber who says they don't know everything,
Or a Dubliner belting out God Save The King.

Like a school swimming teacher not wearing a tag,
Or a Polish grandma with a big rainbow flag.

Like a family planner in a red MAGA hat,
Or a seamless conversion from Adobe Acrobat.

Yes, a self-conscious Spaniard is very obscure,
Like Audi drivers who're emotionally mature.
Or an email that starts "Greetings to you my dear"
Not offering millions or a change of career.

A Maltese ski jumper, a Bolivian sea captain
A transcript of the early films of Charlie Chaplin,
A politician from Hungary declaring he's woke,
Or a chap in a tracksuit who's never drunk Coke.

A footballer's wife with a master degree,
A Hollywood actor who's silicone free;
A crazy cat lady whose house doesn't stink,
A glam North Korean – no, that's too far, I think…

A Mediterranean man skilful at sex
No emotional hangups, no prudish complex,
Who doesn't go crying on his mama's shoulder
Good boy, you are a brave little soldier!

A bachelor party off to Liechtenstein
With two cultured virgins from Newcastle-Upon-Tyne.
Or a Japanese tourist who's travelling alone,
On a Flixbus to Burnley without a smartphone.

A blissful Canadian not giving a blank
When a foreigner misguidedly calls them a Yank
Or a Frenchman who laughs when you tell him the gag
That the blue and the red shouldn't be on his flag.

Or Chinese technology that Americans stole,
A white van not driven by a total arsehole.
State employees who work through their lunch break,
A vegetarian who's never yearned for a steak.

So here must I end my provocative thesis
That the self-conscious Spaniard is an endangered species
But there's one even rarer by its own admission,
It's the Spaniard who's actually won Eurovision!

THE ADMINISTRATIVE PROCESSES OF SPAIN AND LUXEMBOURG

Raymond Goslitski

Hello dear council worker, in Valencia I'm new,
I'd like to come and live here, please tell me what to do.
Is that your ticket number? We're up to ninety-two.
Yours is ninety, so you've missed your position in the queue.
But I'm sitting at your desk now, the lady let me in.
That's not how this procedure works, go back and start again.

Hello again dear worker, I did it right this go,
Please explain procedures, as I'd really love to know…
Tell me what the reason is for your visit today.
Then we can facilitate your own demand to stay.
I'd like to enter both myself and my family
On the local register of this here lovely city.
(predatory smile)

Can I see your passport and your children's birth certificates?
And their passports too with photocopies made in triplicate?
Do you have a proof of residence in Spain – original?
As well as your work contract, signed, the version unabridged an' all?
(frown)

Let me see what I have got – my ID card's right here…
Let me stop you, sir, the passport's legally binding here.
But I'm an EU citizen, we don't have books with pages,
Furthermore just getting one is gonna take me ages!
In order to fulfil this there might be another way
Forget the passport, get instead a shiny new NIE.

In order to get one of those, it's really quite a cinch.
Log on to the website of the police so you can clinch
A meeting at the cop shop where they'll get your paper sorted
And find if you're the type who really needs to be deported.
Thanks again, I'll go and get a NIE right away.
And return with that there document in just one or two days.

Mmmmyes…

Hello dear gestoría, in Valencia I'm new,
I'd like to get a NIE, please tell me what to do.

Hello dear victim, I mean Hi potential customer,
Pay a sweet three hundred and I'll maybe call you "sir".
Give me your exact name as it reads on your ID,
And address and date of birth I promise, lawfully!

Here are all my details, stranger, to whom I place my trust
To get my NIE sorted so I can obtain my…
…just
A moment, while I process all the documents you passed,
I'll be in touch within three weeks if I've been able to ask.
I'm not sure where you'll need to go but hopefully not far,
You'll get a police appointment – by the way, you have a
car…?

NIE, faéééé, wherever you aéééé…

Dear client, it took a little time, I'm sorry for the wait,
But I got you an appointment Friday week at five past eight.
Oh thanks a lot, I was starting to wonder where you'd gone!
Don't get too excited, it's up near to Castellón.
Wait outside the police station at exactly five past eight,
And out of nowhere will appear the holder of your fate.

Hello dear NIE agent, in Valencia I'm new,
Escort me in the police station and tell me what to do.
Good morning Señor Applicant, just sit down over there.
Of course I will, I just can't wait to finish this nightmare.
(wry smile)
Did you get the documents all copied for the list?
Of course! I'm not about to take that stupid bloody risk!
Here is your NIE signed and printed out for you to keep.
Do you have a tissue? I think I'm about to weep!

Hello dear council worker, my NIE has come through,
I'd like to get us registered, please tell me what to do.
Now you have your NIE, we'll put you in the list.
I've brought all other documents, I think I've got the gist!
This seems to be in order, just a moment while I vanish
Oh wait, these birth certificates aren't written out in Spanish…

Hello dear sworn translator, in Valencia I'm fairly new,
I'd like these birth certificates translated well by you.
That will be no problem, I charge you by the word.
I thought you had a template set, at least that's what I heard.
I find it funny that they can't decipher dates and names
In English, Dutch or Albanian, it's all the bloody same!

If you mean the council staff, it's all just control freakery.
None of them have any time for critical thinking geekery.
How much do I owe you for translating these three pages,
With all the same words clearly listed 'cept for names and ages?
That's thirty euro for the document then times by three,
Ninety euro for just thirty minutes' work, **** me!

Hello dear council worker, I've got the docs translated,
It's four months since this bloody process was initiated!
Why don't you call the process by its Spanish-themed design?
'Cos empadronamiento takes up half a bloody line!
That seems to be in order now, I'll print your registrations,
And now you're ready to do all the other administration!
Like what? I thought that that was it, I'm listed everywhere.
Oh no, dear boy, let me explain, sit back down on the chair.
Just do the same again to get yourself a bank account,
Your public health insurance and your tax is paramount.
Make sure you change the registration of your motor car
And get your Spanish driving licence before you go too far.

Hello dear council worker, I've come to sign back out.
But it was just a month ago we got it brought about!
I know, but my employer fired me from my last position,

Because I always took time off to sort out my admission!
I've got a job in Luxembourg, I'll fly out on the first,
I'll have to do this all again, I fear the bloody worst.

Hello dear council worker, in Luxembourg I'm new,
I'd like to come and live here, please tell me what to do.
First, I make your number and then you get your code,
I'll send you all your papers that you can just download.
Everything to live here is automatically assigned
As if you'd been in Luxembourg since nineteen sixty-nine.

THE DAILY RANT: GETTING THREE YOUNG CHILDREN TO SCHOOL THEN HEADING TO THE OFFICE

Raymond Goslitski

All right everyone, it's time, start putting on your shoes.
It's coming up to quarter to nine, there's not a sec to lose!
Yes, that's very funny, with your shirt on upside-down,
But now I'm going out the door, oh no, don't pull that frown!

Please stop crying, I'm not really leaving you behind,
But I ask you get your shoes on now, if you don't flipping mind!
Okay, we have one fully dressed and holding her backpack.
Oh, what d'you mean you've already eaten your midmorning sodding snack?!

Just get your bloody shoes on, and I'll make another sandwich,
Yes dear, I'll be sure that I will wisely mind my language!

What's up now? You've got your brother's socks wedged in your knickers?
And why's my laptop screen now covered in fairy and pony stickers?!

No, I will not just calm right down, I've got a class on Teams
At ten o'clock, now Tinkerbell's a student so it seems…
Go and press the lift button while mum gets on her coat,
Take Peppa out your mouth before she blocks your bloody throat!

The lift is here, let's all get in, I'll get out the car keys,
Oh bugger, now we're heading upwards, this will be a squeeze…
Sorry, there's no room in here for just a single slot,
I know it's just you and your dog, but the Tardis this is not!

Honestly, what cheek, who does he think we bloody are?
We're here now, please stop ramming Paw Patrol stuff on that car!
The door's unlocked, so get inside and sit down in your spots,
Bless you! Bloody hell, my trouser leg's awash with snot!

We're in. If we leave now, we'll be just fifteen minutes late.
That's not too bad, considering the record's forty-eight!
The gate is slowly opening, like watching drying plaster,
Why don't we just get out and walk? I'm sure it would be faster.

Sorry dear, I know you hate it when I show my feelings.
I promise to keep them in check so you don't hit the ceiling.
Yes, I know you're such a goody, never agitated,
Except with me, but that of course is completely unrelated!

So on the motorway we'll go in a couple of short minutes,
Once we pass this camper van I'll have to break the limit.
For what it's worth, the speed cam's never on in Alboraya,
It doesn't really matter if your velocity is higher!

Look behind, a single driver in the carpool lane!
I'll slow right down until it makes the bastard think again!
Oh yes, that's great you tosser, overtaking on the right,
I'll show you what I think of you by flashing my headlights!

It doesn't really help to go much faster anyway,
Because of that there traffic jam that greets us every day.
Here are the traffic lights and look, he's just two cars in front,

Did you think this was a race, you stupid f… *(sorry)*

Here we are, now all get out, I'll go and park somewhere,
And don't forget your backpacks – damn, I left them on the chair!
Well never mind, at least you've got all your mid-morning snacks,
Oh, wait a minute, no you don't, they're still in your backpacks!

Well, have a lovely day, won't you? Don't look at me that way,
I'm not the only one who gets distracted in the fray!
Look, close the door, there's going to be a free spot opposite,
Too bloody late, that bastard in the van has taken it!

I'll drive once round the block and pick you up again, that's best,
And then we can go off to work to have a bloody rest.
The dire lack of parking spaces here makes me despair,
And now the kids are safe in school, I properly can swear!

Oh where the fucking hell is she? My fourth time round the block,

That batty old Kartoffelkopf is getting on my cock!
Oh there she is, the liar, now I truly understand,
She's perched there on the corner with a coffee in her hand!

Get in, get in, I see you didn't piss away a minute
Procuring a cup for single use with steaming brown stuff in it!
While I go round and round the block you think I work for free?
Well you can have lunch on your – oh, you got the drink for me…

(awkward silence)

Pwhhhh…

I see the lights are red again for a generous interval,
And look, that blue Mercedes has already begun to crawl!
The pedestrian light is red, that's all, we should still be in station,
These Spaniards really see these traffic signs as decoration!

Here we are, I'll drop you off and go and park the car,
It's Thursday, so it's market day, I'll likely drive quite far.

I don't have long, my online course won't start unless I'm there,
Oh shit, I think my laptop's with the bags upon the chair!

Bah never mind, I'll give the seminar over my phone,
So let's get on, this car won't find a space all on its own.
Just a minute, I'm alone in this here pile of crap,
Let's get up to some mischief in this fifteen-minute rap

I'm Raymond Gee,
Yeah yeah that's me,
Alone in the car baby
Goin' pretty far,
Got fifteen precious minutes
To make some trouble in it
Take off all my…

Oh hold on…

That should be fifteen minute *gap*. Not rap, gap. Sorry.

Oh look, a Fiat driver with Italian licence plates,
Those people with their patriotic sentiment are great.
They put their love of homeland selflessly in first position,

Above their and their family's own safety – great tradition!

Found a space about five hundred metres from my work,
I made it all the way here without looking like a jerk!
Hi Michelle, how was your journey in? Oh, great to hear,
Mine was really nice, a lovely drive this time of year.

I'm sorry, I can't hang around I've got a seminar
And I'm late because I had to park out fairly far.
Connect to Teams and here I am, I'm sorry that I'm late,
Oh shit, it was tomorrow, I've confused the bloody dates!

A SENSE OF CATS

Cate Baum

We would like to think the muse is pushing the subconscious to create; some disembodied spirit that is you, a shadow person waiting at our back to whisper the path of the brush or the knife, the tapping of keys, the trace of the pencil. A possession of expression, to the fingers to the paint, to the cut, to the rubbing of colours and shade, to the movement of bodies, to the stillness required, to the ritual of creation. We summon these directions, from nowhere we know in this world, but rather, from another place we know both intimately and not at all.

Artificial intelligence is pushing in, people were saying, to ruin art forever. Computers taking over the planet to form soulless inorganic works that have nothing to do with the human experience. But in my case, as a creative, I found myself wanting to corrupt that idea, and take it over myself, and use AI as a tool to create art. And so I download an AI generation software to create images.

The thing about AI is that it is simply code. Written by humans, a binary yes/no scenario. 1 or zero seems like only two choices, but by lining up 1,0 over and over again you get sequences. 01111010000101. As with anything, the nuance of sequences becomes what you are hunting down for elegance.

And with AI, machine learning is working unendingly to improve its nuances of sequences: as we speak, AI has read all the new stuff all of us just posted and uploaded in a second. And again. And again. What sequence can you put inside another sequence, to fill it with zeros and ones in a different formation? In this way, anything is possible to be learned by a machine, down to the fractal, quantum sequence of all things. And everything, generated by any prompt, will be entirely unique due to the constant updating of information that we, the humans, are feeding it, making its neurons connect like an invisible dance of exactly what we accuse it of not having: the human experience.

How does it work? Take an example of a cat. The first time you ask your AI to draw a cat by writing a prompt to be generated, the AI has only the references at that exact moment in time on the whole internet to draw a cat.

Your instruction might be "Cat", and you'll get the AI's best guess from that information. But the AI has never met a cat. It only has a sense of cats. But I have seen a cat, and loved one, and held one, and all the things.

I must now describe it to my AI in words it can use. A sense of words.

A cat jumping over a gate with a white bib, I try.

What I get is a cat jumping over a gate. The gate is wearing a white bib you get in America when you eat ribs and gravy.

A cat playing with a ball of wool

What I get is a cat playing with a football, made of knitted wool

A cat with long claws

What I get is a cat with long claws… coming out of its eyeballs

A cat cleaning itself

What I get is a cat with a broom, brushing itself with six paws and two tails, I guess, to suggest motion?

I have to write a summoning spell of the cat I want, like a magician in a chalk circle calling to demons to appear. I am calling on my muses of the AI, to the four cardinal corners of Chat GPT, Elon Musk, TikTok, and Wikipedia to bring forth the materialisation of the demon known as CAT. This sigil must describe the cat so definitively that no errors can be made in its appearance on my screen.

I cannot use words that have no physical sense, no literal visual reference. For example, I cannot use the phrase "inherently regal". I would get the sense of those words, and what they relate to, a cat wearing a crown that looks a bit like Prince William maybe. I cannot say "an obstinate cat" or "an ordinary cat." Because these words need reference, a sliding scale. An AI cannot judge what an ordinary cat is to me without basing its judgement on all the cats on the internet and then my opinion, but my opinion is not inside the internet. It's in my head. That's why I have to create the most perfect summoning prompt.

And so, to paint a cat is to paint a very basic sense of a cat, which can be variated and tweaked, and the prompt to write to do such a thing is so very close to a spell, to a magical ritual, that I started thinking about what old-time spells actually were.

Were magicians and witches in history using specially formed sounds and chants made of words that gave the other world the tools to put together the creatures they were summoning? Were the symbols drawn on the ground a sequence of prompts in some language we used to know in an ancient technology, but have long since forgotten?

What is AI, but the same lightning fast yes/no decision making we all make every microsecond of our lives? Are we also AI? Is the muse we all feel when we create… a person… somewhere else… outside of this virtual reality…typing a prompt into their computer to generate…us?

An overweight blonde woman in her fifties stands on a neon-lit stage in a Spanish city, wearing a black skirt and glittering boots. She is reading, in English, a story about the realisation of where everything came from and what reality is.

GENERATE PROMPT

ABOUT CLUB HEMINGWAY VLC

Club Hemingway is the original and free-to-enter American-style literary open mic event for English-speaking writers who live in Valencia to come and read their work aloud to a crowd of friendly listeners.

Monthly Thursdays at Radio City Valencia

@clubhemingwayvlc

https://www.meetup.com/club-hemingway-literary-open-mic/

Printed in Great Britain
by Amazon

44374486R00078